BAKING WITH DAD

AURORA CACCIAPUOTI

Today is a special day because...

...I am baking with **Dad!**

We already have all the ingredients.
It's important to choose them carefully!

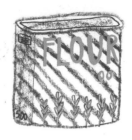

Let's start.

Then add the sugar!

Woo-hoo!

And now:

Mix! Mix!

Shake!

Shake!

Whisk!

Whisk!

Next, flour.

LOTS of it!

Then, we need
butter and milk, right?

We'll need lots of fruit
to finish off our creation!

Be patient. Let the magic begin!

Time to decorate!

Ding - dong!

Quick! Quick!

"Dad, are we going to bake again next week?"